This Little Tiger book belongs to:

_____

_____

_____

For my good friends, Sharon and Ian
~ S. C.

For you, Pa, with love
~ G. H.

LITTLE TIGER PRESS
1 The Coda Centre, 189 Munster Road, London SW6 6AW
www.littletiger.co.uk

First published in Great Britain 2006
by Little Tiger Press, London

This edition published 2013

Printed in China • LTP/1900/0679/0613

2 4 6 8 10 9 7 5 3 1

By the Light of the Moon

Sheridan Cain   Gaby Hansen

LITTLE TIGER PRESS

The moon
shone bright
in the evening
sky as Mother Mouse
watched over Little Mouse.
He lay curled and snuggly tight,
a grassy nook for his bed. High
above, a starry blanket twinkled
silver bright.

"Sleep tight, Little Mouse,"
she whispered.

Mole tumbled through the hedge, tripping over Mother Mouse.

"Mother Mouse," he said, "you cannot leave your baby there. The farmer is coming to plow the field. That bed's not safe."

"Oh, dear," said Mother Mouse, hugging Little Mouse close. "Where can my Little Mouse sleep?"

"Perhaps his bed should be underground," said Mole. "That's where Little Mouse could sleep."

So Mother Mouse
scritched and
scratched the
soft earth.

Soon the hole was
deep, and she tucked
Little Mouse into his
new bed.

Little Mouse snuggled down, but he could not settle. There was no moon. "Mama," he cried, "it's so dark, I cannot sleep."

Owl, watching from the willow tree, heard Little Mouse cry. He flew down.

"Mother Mouse," he said, "that bed is much too dark for Little Mouse."

"Oh, my," said Mother Mouse. "Where can my Little Mouse sleep?"

"Perhaps where the moon is brighter," said Owl. "Up there in the tree is where Little Mouse could sleep."

Mother Mouse scrambled
onto the branch of the
willow. She spied an empty
nest, and placed Little Mouse in
his new bed. Little Mouse snuggled down, but the wind
was strong and his bed felt wobbly.

"Mama," he cried, "I'm dizzy! It's very high up here.
I might fall out."

Duck awoke—she had
heard Little Mouse cry.
"Mother Mouse," she
called, "that bed is far
too high for Little Mouse."
"Oh, dear me!" said
Mother Mouse. "Where
can my Little Mouse sleep?"
"A bed of reeds would
be nice and cozy," said
Duck. "That's where
Little Mouse could sleep."

So Mother Mouse
took Little Mouse
to the river's edge.

She hopped and
jumped and flattened
the reedy leaves . . .

then placed Little Mouse in his new bed. Little Mouse snuggled down, but soon he felt cold. "Mama," he cried, "I don't like this squishy, squashy bed. It's damp, and I might sink."

Mother
Mouse
carried
Little Mouse
back to the riverbank.
Hugging him tight,
she hung her head
and sighed. "Where,
oh where, can my
Little Mouse sleep?"

She looked
into Little Mouse's eyes.
They sparkled bright in
the soft light of the moon.
Mother Mouse looked
up at the moon, and the
moon winked back at her.
Mother Mouse smiled.

She thought back to when she was small. She remembered her mother's bright eyes watching over her. She remembered her blanket of silver stars. And she remembered the soft light of the moon shining above her.

Mother Mouse looked toward the field
that had been her home since she was tiny.
Her eyes sparkled. The farmer had been,
but in the shelter of the big tree, her home
was safe.

Mother Mouse carried
Little Mouse back to
his old bed. She laid
him gently down. Little
Mouse snuggled tight.

"Mother," he yawned,
"this is my bed—it's
just right."

"Of course it is,"
said Mother Mouse,
smiling. "Sleep tight,
Little Mouse."